THE A-TEAM™*

annual

£2.99

Contents

Copyright© MCMLXXXIV by Stephen J. Cannell Productic
All rights reserved throughout the world.
Published in Great Britain by
World International Publishing Limited,
P.O. Box 111, Great Ducie Street, Manchester M60 3B
Printed in Italy.
SBN 7235 6717 4.

*a trademark of Stephen J. Cannell Productions and
licensed by Merchandising Corporation of America, In

SWAMP WRECK

The Face Man adjusted his clerical collar, stepped out of the swamp, and approached the lonely cabin. To his right, dead fish were drying over a fire. As he neared the cabin the canvas over the doorway was pulled to one side and the face of a toothless old woman appeared.

Face grinned his best travelling salesman's grin.

"Do you feel life is passing you by?" he asked.

The woman's expression didn't waver.

"Do you feel somehow 'different' to other people? Do some folks think you're strange?"

Face was now close enough to smell the piles of animal skins by the doorway. He cranked up his smile a notch or two and persevered.

"You see, we believe that if you are what other, less enlightened folk might call abnormal, you might be onto something – it could be because you are actually better than the others. And we at the Self Help Hypno School – dedicated to better living through positive thought – are prepared to offer you one whole year's free subscription to our very own magazine, and all we require in return is . . ." Here Face checked a small piece of paper in his trouser pocket, ". . . about twenty feet of tubular aluminium piping, a large sheet of industrial silk and some snake bite serum. What do you say? A deal?"

Face heard some clicking noises inside the cabin and the woman drew the canvas further back to reveal a small, heavily bearded man loading the second barrel of a double-barrelled shotgun. As he snapped it shut and took aim, Face turned and ran, splashing through the murky swamp waters as shotgun pellets peppered the huge cottonwood trees around him.

It had been that kind of day. Only two hours previously, after springing a bishop held by South American terrorists, they had been relaxing on board a Dakota provided by Howling Mad Murdock. They were somewhere over Louisiana when Sue noticed smoke pouring from the engine on the port wing. When the propeller stopped, Face checked out with Murdock.

"Where did you get this bus anyway?" Face asked.

Murdock took his harmonica out of his mouth and wiped it on his trousers. "From a film lot," he said. "Some World War II movie. *Frankenstein Joins the Army* is the working title."

"Didn't you check out the plan?"

"Let's say this one's been modified," said Murdock. "For a start, there's extra buttons and switches and things. Like this thing here." Murdock flipped a switch on the controls, there was a huge explosion from the starboard engine and the ancient plane began losing height rapidly.

"This plane's rigged, dummy," said Face. "It's a prop for the film, wired to explode!"

"How would I know that?" asked Murdock. "Don't forget, I'm crazy. Where are we?"

Face looked down at the endless forest of cottonwood trees below. "Swamp land," he said grimly.

"Then get back in there and strap yourself down. This might tickle a bit."

An eerie silence settled on the A-Team as the Dakota glided over the tops of the cottonwood trees. When Murdock spotted an open stretch of water he tried to put her down.

In a flurry of dirty spray and tearing metal, the Dakota aquaplaned across the water while Murdock wrestled with the controls. The water slowed the Dakota but didn't stop it, and suddenly the space ran out and they were plunging through the trees.

Within seconds, both wings had been ripped off. The fuselage bounced once, rolled, broke open, then stopped.

They were shaken, but no bones were broken. Hannibal had dragged B.A. out of the wreckage and was beginning to revive him when Sue screamed. They turned to see Sue clutching a small wound on her calf, while a deadly moccasin snake slithered into the tangle of roots at the bottom of a nearby tree.

A search of the plane revealed plenty of stage and film props — including a giant wind machine — but no serum. It was then that the Face Man had gone on his woefully unsuccessful mission to the cabin.

Back at the wreck, B.A. was muttering angrily to himself as he placed a metal rod in the cleft of a tree and bent it into shape. Murdock was removing the engine from a flat bottomed boat he had found nearby.

"Wouldn't it be better just taking the boat?" asked Face, on his return.

Hannibal shook his head. "Sue's getting worse and it could take us months to find our way out in a boat."

"Won't anybody mind?"

As if in answer to the Face's question there was a sharp crack, followed by a creaking sound, and as a cottonwood toppled down towards them, a fusillade of rifle fire opened up from the forest. As he dived out of the way of the crashing tree Hannibal saw several shadowy figures fanning out in the thickening mist. Grabbing his machine gun and several pistols from the wreck, he told the others of his intentions.

"They're hunters — I'm going to be the game. I'll buy you some time — so use it."

"Who are those guys?" asked B.A.

"Hasn't anyone told them I've

got a low threshold of death?" said Murdock indignantly.

Hannibal put two clips of ammunition in his belt and shrugged.

"Maybe they think we're tax collectors," he said. "Or maybe we busted their still. Who knows? Maybe they think the war's still going on."

Hannibal smiled briefly and then, running quickly from side to side at a crouch, he set off to present a tempting target to his pursuers.

While Hannibal was using up a good deal of the many tricks he had learned for staying alive, B.A. was bolting and taping a frame together, using fuel and water

pipes from the wreck. Face was measuring out strips of cloth he had cut from a parachute, and Murdock was fixing up the boat's outboard motor to the wind machine. Sue sat slumped against a piece of the fuselage, shivering violently.

"You think this is going to work?" asked Face, when they finally carried the completed craft to the water's edge. B.A. glared at him as they placed it in the boat and strapped Sue into her seat. There was a slight bluish tinge round her mouth and her breathing was becoming increasingly irregular. Murdock switched the motor on and the giant blades of the wind machine

whirred into action.

"If we can get up the speed on the water we're home free," he said.

Face and B.A. gave the boat a shove.

After taxiing round the edge of the stretch of water, Murdock gave it full power and the flat-bottomed boat picked up speed. As the trees on the other side loomed closer, Murdock saw a rifle in the bushes, aimed directly at him. He pulled hard on the controls and the motorised hang-glider lifted agonisingly slowly from the speeding boat, dipped once across the surface of the thick green water, then soared high up above the treetops and into the sky, leaving only the echo of lunatic laughter, and the tinny drone of the engine as it carried them away.

Back on the ground, the Face Man's elation was interrupted by a shuffling in the undergrowth beside him and the hooting of an owl. Hannibal appeared, smiling but dirty.

"You bin watching too many cowboy films, Hannibal," said B.A.

"I know it," Hannibal agreed, "and right now we should be circling the wagons. I reckon they'll try and hit us again before dark. If we can scare 'em off till the sun goes down we can slip away."

"Slip away where?" asked B.A.

"You remember that time when we hid out near here, when we had to bust out?"

"You mean when I got shot in the hand?" asked Face.

"And I got the clothes burned off my back?" B.A. chipped in.

Hannibal nodded and smiled into his friends' worried faces.

"We'll use the same plan," he said. "We should get the hang of it this time. Come nightfall we'll be safe."

"How can you be so sure?" the Face Man queried.

"Why, didn't you know . . ." said Hannibal, relighting his cigar, "Indians never attack at night."

It was dusk when the attack came and B.A., Face and Hannibal had spent the time well, preparing for it. Further investigation of the crashed plane's curious cargo had brought to light several explosive flares, gas-guns that fired red paint balls designed to burst on target, a thousand rounds of blank ammunition, two rubber knives, a machine that made a noise like a ricochet, a box full of stick-on scars, and a gorilla mask. B.A. was putting some leaves over one of several holes he had dug when the leading attackers triggered a flare charge with a trip wire to signal the beginning of the fight.

Hannibal immediately opened up with a barrage of blanks and Murdock loosed off some paint balls, causing a great deal of confusion among the men he hit.

B.A. cut a rope that held a small

tree bent double, and a shower of sharpened sticks rained on the attackers. Carefully placed flares exploded with ear-splitting bangs and the ricochet machine worked overtime. To the hunters, who were expecting minimal resistance, it all came as quite a shock. When a spiked weight on a rope was swung among them, they began to scatter.

"Come back!" yelled one of the men, standing firm. As he stepped resolutely forward his foot caught in a concealed noose, and he was swung high into the air where he remained, hanging upside down. Two others rushing to rescue him disappeared down one of the holes B.A. had dug.

More flares exploded, Murdock scored three consecutive direct hits with his paint balls, and when Hannibal rushed forward, firing continuously from the hip, the rest of the attackers scattered.

Hannibal cut the man down from the tree, and after checking that the men in the hole couldn't get out, demanded an explanation.

"You don't know?" asked the man, genuinely surprised. He stood around 5 feet 10 inches, wore a beard and a black wool cap. He looked like he was peering through a hedge.

"We don't know," said Hannibal.

"My son got shot this morning. The girl with him said a bunch of men did it. We figured it was you."

"Is he dead?" asked Hannibal. The man shook his head.

"Nope. Not yet, anyhow. We daren't move him, though — he's weak."

Hannibal drew his pistol and placed it at the base of the man's spine.

"Take us to him," he said.

"You're crazier than Murdock, man!" snarled B.A. "We're talking survival here!"

"You got it," smiled Hannibal. "But didn't you ever see the film where the army doctor saves the chief's son?"

"I saw it," said the Face Man. "But we're not in the army any more — this guy's no chief — and you aren't a doctor."

"Hey," said Hannibal, pushing the man ahead of him, "why can't you guys think positive?"

They reached the man's village around midnight. With Hannibal keeping his pistol pressed in the man's back, they walked slowly down a corridor of heavily armed men to the shack where the wounded boy lay ill. A quick examination by Hannibal told him the bullet was lodged near the spine. Any sudden movement could paralyse the boy for ever.

The door burst open and a skinny little man with a large cowboy hat came in, dragging a young girl with him.

"Are these the men?" he barked.

The girl's frightened eyes studied the three members of the A-Team. Face smiled uneasily. B.A. winked quickly then continued glaring. Hannibal smiled.

"Tell the truth now, girl," he said kindly. "Nobody's been killed yet and we can save this boy's life if you let us."

The girl's eyes filled with tears as she looked down at the boy in the bed.

"I didn't mean anyone to get hurt," she said. "It was an accident. The gun went off when he was showing me how it should be loaded. I knew if he died I'd be blamed. I didn't expect them to find anyone else round here. I'm sorry — really sorry."

She put her hands to her face

and burst out crying. Hannibal knelt and stroked her hair.

"It's ok," he said.

"No, it isn't."

The voice was cold, hard and firm. It came from behind the beard of a tall fat man in a coonskin cap. Hannibal rose to face him. On tiptoe he was level with the necklace of animal bones the man wore on his chest. The man carried a big club.

"Ever thought of taking up wrestling?" Hannibal asked. The man grabbed him by the front of his clothes and lifted him into the air with one hand.

"I don't like jokes," he said simply. Hannibal chewed his cigar. "And this thing has gone too far. You killed two of our men."

"No, they're not dead," interrupted the Face Man eagerly. "They're in a hole back near the plane. They'll be a bit wet but they're alive. Honestly. Really . . . truly."

"I don't believe you. I say our only chance is to get rid of these three and hide the bodies."

As B.A. stepped forward, the man felled him with one tremendous blow of his club.

There were murmurs of admiration and assent from the crowd that had gathered.

"What about the boy?" asked Hannibal.

"You won't be alive to worry about that."

In the distance, Hannibal heard the faint buzz of an approaching helicopter. He lifted his gun hand and placed the pistol to his captor's temple.

"Listen good, death-breath," he said, still smiling. "When that chopper lands we're gonna take that boy to hospital and we're going too. Nobody's been killed yet, but you try and stop us and you'll get the big cigar and somewhere new to put it."

The man in the coonskin cap looked round the room. The thick night air grew more tense as the helicopter came closer and closer. Eventually, the boy's father broke the silence.

"Put him down," he said. "We'll do as he says."

Hannibal was lowered gently to the ground and he went outside to

wave Murdock down. Standing in the helicopter's spotlight as the wind sent piles of dead leaves flying into the air around him, Hannibal could hear Murdock's voice shouting above the roar of the engines.

"Sue's o.k.," he yelled. "She's a tough old bird. So tough, buddy, that the doctors sent me back to see how the snake is!"

They loaded the boy carefully onto the chopper and made room for his father to sit down. B.A., still unconscious, was laid alongside him. Hannibal and Face Man climbed aboard and signalled Murdock to take off.

"Where did you get this one?" asked Face as the chopper rose noisily into the night skies. "It's not another flying joke shop, is it?"

"I'm crazy, not stupid," Murdock replied. "This here's a mean machine. A numero uno."

"Where did you get it?" Face persisted.

"At the airport. Some bigwig was coming around. I just told the pilot I wanted to clear his chopper for security reasons. Did you notice the seal on the door?"

"The Seal! Murdock, you're crazy!"

"Thanks."

As Murdock and the Face Man argued, the wounded boy's father drew Hannibal's attention to the pistol he was still holding.

"Would you have used it?" he asked.

Hannibal pointed the pistol at the back of Murdock's head. "I don't see why not," he said, pulling the trigger.

The man stiffened as the hammer came down, but instead of a bullet, a wooden stick came racing out of the barrel, stopped, and a small flag unfurled beneath. In beg red letters on a yellow background the word BANG had been written.

The man laughed and Hannibal joined in. When Face and Murdock saw what had happened they joined in too. Even the boy managed a smile, and though none of the others ever thought to mention it to him, B.A.'s body shook a little, and Hannibal could have sworn he heard the sound of suppressed laughter coming from his supposedly unconscious friend.

HANNIBAL

As we are so often reminded, the A-Team leader, John 'Hannibal' Smith, just loves the jazz. Cool and dangerous as a charmed cobra, Hannibal would rather play baseball with a live hand grenade than find out the secrets of life inside a coffin. Crazy enough to try and sell striped paint to a zebra, Hannibal's act is so tight that in Vietnam he was a well-respected Colonel right up to the moment – four days after the war – that he wandered out of the DMZ with 100 million yen belonging to the Bank of Hanoi. When Hannibal learnt his only alibi was dead, he and his men chose running rather than staying to beat the rap. They're running still . . .

14

B.A.

Bosco Baracus is the name his mother gave him, but to the rest of us and to the A-Team themselves he's plain B.A. In South East Asia, where he earned his reputation for having a Bad Attitude, B.A. was recognised as the finest field infantry mechanic in the military. But times change. Big and bad, and with jewels hanging off him like lights on a Christmas tree, B.A. is now known as an electronics wizard who could build a racing car from a sackful of bottle tops and a rubber band. Like Achilles, B.A. has a weakness: fear of flying. He knows it's irrational, but like he says: "If it's safer to fly than drive – how come they don't put parachutes in cars?"

When the War Came Back

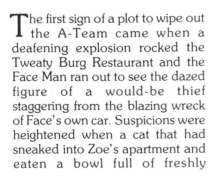

The first sign of a plot to wipe out the A-Team came when a deafening explosion rocked the Tweaty Burg Restaurant and the Face Man ran out to see the dazed figure of a would-be thief staggering from the blazing wreck of Face's own car. Suspicions were heightened when a cat that had sneaked into Zoe's apartment and eaten a bowl full of freshly delivered prawns was found seriously ill from a massive overdose of arsenic.

And then B.A. woke from a violent brawl to find himself in a strange car with the doors welded shut, moving slowly along a conveyor belt towards an automatic car-crushing machine. It was only by smashing his fists through the windscreen and cutting his ropes on the broken glass that he was able to escape.

After this incident, Hannibal decided he needed a close shave of his own, and made his way down to Mo's Hair Port.

Mo Cropper had opened his Hair Port after the pop group he had been managing left to join a fringe religious cult on the final day of their last and least successful tour. Mo stood 6 feet 7 inches tall, wore a frilly silk cowboy shirt, a top hat, and a large gold ring through his nose. He smiled when Hannibal walked into his salon and flopped down on the chair. Mo smiled at everybody.

"Hannibal," he said in his deep, mellifluous, accent-free voice, "it's so good to see you. I presume you want your image updating?"

"Just a trim," said Hannibal.

"I'm afraid that would necessitate the removal of your hat."

"Make that a shave – and afterwards, we'll talk."

"Of course."

Mo wrapped a hot towel round Hannibal's face, leaving a hole for the cigar. He worked up some lather in a metal cup, and was stropping his open razor when he caught sight of two men in the doorway. Both had guns trained on him. One was smiling. The other held a finger to his lips. They motioned Mo away from Hannibal. Mo reluctantly complied.

While one man held Mo in a back room of the salon, the other made ready to shave Hannibal. Standing behind the A-Team leader, he removed the hot towel, applied the lather, then leant forward with the open razor in his hand.

"I hope it's sharp," said Hannibal. "I can't stand a dull blade."

The man smiled and placed the razor to Hannibal's neck. There was a loud click from under the sheet protecting Hannibal's clothing.

"I can't stand a nervous barber either," said Hannibal, puffing on his cigar. "I don't like to see a man's hands shake when he's shaving me. One little nick and I'm liable to do something nasty."

The man felt the cold touch of metal pushing against his stomach.

"You're bluffing," he said.

"Who sent you?" asked Hannibal.

"I can't tell you."

"You've got no choice."

"Bodene."

"Thanks. Now, shave!"

As the man nervously scraped Hannibal's whiskers, Hannibal began to realise the trouble he was in. In South East Asia, Bodene had been almost a myth to most regular soldiers. Average height with clean-cut good looks and the kind of manners you might expect from a college major, Bodene's record under fire was the stuff of legends,

his reputation for bringing his men home second to none.

And then, in an action in the jungle near the DMZ, an action in which Hannibal himself had taken part, Bodene's men had suffered terrible casualties and Bodene had disappeared. There had been rumours that he'd changed sides, that he'd turned rogue and was conducting his own private war,

that he'd been shipped back to the U.S. in a straight jacket. Nobody who knew what had happened would talk, so the tales of Bodene's awesome fighting powers grew as each of his exploits was embroidered and added to by the tellers

"You missed a bit under my nose," said Hannibal, when the man intimated that he had finished shaving him. The man duly scraped off the offending tuft.

"Where is he?" asked Hannibal, standing up and rubbing his chin.

As the sheet fell away the man saw that the weapon Hannibal had threatened him with was not a gun at all, but the empty metal tube of a cigar holder. His face contorted with fury.

"Why, you –" He raised the razor above his head, but Hannibal decked him with a hard right to the solar plexus and a left cross to the chin.

At the same instant Mo appeared from the back room, carrying the other gunman by the scruff of the neck.

"Still keeping bad company, I see," drawled Mo.

"This one might have a future as a prison barber," said Hannibal, as he searched the man on the floor.

Mo frisked his captive and they were about to call the police when the phone rang.

"Hello. This is Zoe. I'm thinking of taking some pachyderms over a European mountain range and I wondered if there was anyone there who could give me some advice."

"I'm your man," said Hannibal.

"Good. Listen – I'm at the paper and Eldridge is throwing a fit. We've got an anonymous tip that there's been a large scale theft at the army base. Plenty heavy duty firepower and – get this – a tank."

"It could be a hoax," said Hannibal.

"And maybe pigs will fly," said Zoe. "Lynch has been onto the paper. He wants Eldridge to hush it up. He thinks it's you."

"Okay, Zoe, you know what to do."

"Sure, where are you going to go?"

Hannibal studied the drinks bill he had lifted from his attacker's wallet.

"Paddy's Bar. It's on the waterfront."

"You could hide an awful lot of machinery in the warehouses there."

"Exactly."

Hannibal put down the phone, used Mo's mirrors to disguise himself as Mr Lee from the Chinese laundry, then made his way down to Paddy's Bar.

After a couple of drinks and a couple of innocent sounding questions that were met with icy silence, Hannibal left Paddy's Bar to scout around the mouldering warehouses that surrounded it. When he was climbing an old metal drainpipe to reach an interesting looking window, the pipe suddenly came away from its rotten holdings and Hannibal fell backwards, tumbling some twenty feet to the ground.

As he struggled to his feet a hooded man stepped out of the shadows with a baseball bat, and two seconds later Hannibal was lying unconscious in an oily puddle.

At the Veterans Administrations

Hospital, Face and Zoe, posing as emissaries from the Surgeon General of the Air Force, were hustling Murdock out of his room under a barrage of questions and the baffled protests of Nurse Schnider.

"He's fading in and out again," explained Face, pushing Murdock along in front of him. "You remember he used to think he was an egg-plant?"

"Yes."

"Now he thinks he's hatched," said Face, taking a notebook out of his pocket and firing a rapid series of questions at Murdock.

"Brain?" he snapped.

"Like a jellyfish in a washing machine," replied Murdock.

"Sense of touch?"

"Gone. I think I've got somebody else's skin on. Look at these hands! They're like plastic gloves full of sticks!"

Face took notes as they neared the front door.

"Gloves full of sticks . . ." he said, writing. "Good. Anything else?"

"Doctor, my eyes – they're like hot mothballs. I think I've caught something off my pet giraffe!"

Face turned sternly to Nurse Schnider.

"Don't tell me this man is allowed a giraffe in his room?" he said.

"It's not her fault," said Murdock. "She doesn't know where I hide it. Nothing's been the same since the last plague of locusts. I blame the doctor, you know."

"Why?"

"He won't believe I can't stop telling lies."

Face pushed Murdock through the front doors of the hospital and, as Zoe signed the release papers, they hurried to where B.A. was waiting in a pick-up truck.

When Zoe joined them they set off for the waterfront.

In a dimly lit warehouse on that same waterfront, Hannibal's head felt like there was a rhinoceros inside trying to get out. The sight in front of him did little to alleviate his discomfort – Bodene in full combat dress, his once handsome face now thin, gaunt, ravaged. Bodene was handcuffing Hannibal to a chain buried deep in a large block of cement.

"You need mustard, not grease-paint – Hammy-Ball!"

"Why are you doing this, Bodene?" asked Hannibal.

Bodene clipped the handcuffs shut. "You sprung that trap too soon in the DMZ," he said, checking Hannibal was completely secure. "The ones that got away got us."

"If we hadn't moved then they'd have all got away. You blew it, Bodene, and you know it."

Bodene's eyes stood out like eggs in the wrong nest.

"You think I don't know that?" he snarled. "You know what they do to you when they capture you alive? Prison scars a man, Smith, like a hot grill scars a fish."

"Why the tank?"

"Some of the boys feel we're getting a raw deal, that people don't take enough notice of us. If we can capture a nuclear power station that should change."

"Are you sure?"

Bodene laughed and the hollow, empty sound rang round the warehouse like a cracked bell.

"Sure I'm sure," he said. "The one I have in mind was built with the usual official farsightedness and regard for safety – slap bang in the middle of the San Andreas Fault!"

Hannibal looked round the warehouse: at Bodene, the tank, four other hooded, armed men, and boxes filled with live ammunition.

"Did your mother never buy you any fireworks as a child?" he asked. "You know what a melt-down along the fault could mean?"

"I know. Bye-bye, baby, bye-bye!"

"You need a doctor, Bodene. You're talking double fried noodles here."

"Don't worry about what I need, Mr Bigshot Hannibal Smith. When we drop you in the bay –"

Suddenly all the lights in the warehouse went out and Hannibal began trying to slip his cuffs. If he had guessed it right, the rest of the A-Team were working the three second light trick. As he heard stealthy footsteps padding past, he was convinced.

The three second light trick had been used by the A-Team on several occasions, and was extremely effective in clearing confined spaces against superior odds.

All that was needed was access to the light source, fast hands, and an ability to count slow under pressure. Once the lights go out, the A-Team go in. When the lights go on – three seconds later – the A-Team start fighting. When the lights go out – another three seconds – the A-Team swiftly move to new positions, new targets.

It was a ruse they had perfected in the heat of battle, and when the

lights came on, Hannibal just had time to see B.A., Face Man and Murdock take out three of Bodene's men with perfectly executed pressure blows to the neck. As they sank unconscious to the floor, the lights, operated by Zoe, were doused again.

Three seconds later, and the lights came on again. Murdock felled the last of Bodene's men and Face chased Bodene onto the tank as B.A. tried to free Hannibal.

"Forget me, Sergeant!" said Hannibal. "Get that tank."

In the darkness, B.A. sped towards the tank. When he had counted to three he pulled the pin from a grenade on his belt and, as the lights came up, he swung up onto the tank's gun barrel and dropped it down the muzzle. Inside, he could hear Bodene clumsily clanking through the gears.

B.A. dropped from his position and went to shield Face Man, who had been struck on the head by Bodene and was lying slumped against a crate of ammunition.

Zoe was still working the lights when the grenade went off, splitting the barrel and starting a fire inside. Bodene leapt out of the turret with his trousers alight.

Murdock put him down with three straight rights and poured a bucket of water over him.

The tank, aflame and out of control, rumbled round the warehouse. After narrowly missing Hannibal, it crunched through a stack full of live ammunition, setting off a hail of bullets that flew at random round the warehouse. It continued on its way, straight through the wall of the warehouse, across a patch of open ground — scattering some of the late arrivals at Paddy's Bar — and, with a deep splash and a hiss like a trainload of angry cats, it fell into the black waters of the bay.

By now the lights were on full time and the fire in the ammunition was getting out of control.

As the flames licked round Hannibal's concrete block he manoeuvred a cigar butt to his lips and used them to light it. B.A. was beside him.

"You're not going to be able to get me free, B.A.," he said calmly.

"Oh yeah, sucker?"

B.A. stood on the concrete block, grabbed hold of the chains where they disappeared into the concrete, and pulled.

"If I know Bodene, there's an anvil in there," said Hannibal, a sudden sadness crossing his face as a stray bullet sent his cigar flying from his mouth.

B.A. ignored him. His muscles, as dark and firm as the tyres on a ten-ton truck, stood out like sculpted coal as he strained to pull the chains free from the concrete.

His face, a mask of ferocious concentration, betrayed none of the pain he was feeling. And then a crack in the concrete appeared, widened, and with a furious last flourish, B.A. pulled Hannibal's chains free. He had just thrown them at Hannibal when another loose bullet grazed his forehead and he fell to the ground as if pole-axed.

Hannibal was dragging him towards the hole the tank had made in the wall when the squeal of tyres outside the door signalled the arrival of Colonel Lynch and his men.

"I'm not your man, Lynch," said Hannibal. "That's Bodene there."

He nodded to where Bodene was struggling to his feet.

"You're not getting away this time, Smith," said Lynch coldly. "There's just no way out!"

Hannibal looked around him. For once, Lynch seemed to be right. Although the rest of the A-Team had escaped, there seemed little hope for Hannibal and B.A.

. . . Until Hannibal heard a whisper through the hole in the wall.

"What's keeping you?" hissed Face. "We're ready to go, man!"

As Face spoke, a box of rocket grenades went up and Lynch and his men threw themselves to the ground. Hannibal lifted B.A. over his shoulder and slipped through the hole in the wall. He was amazed to see Murdock, Zoe and Face waiting for them in the basket of an ancient-looking hydrogen balloon.

Hannibal dropped B.A. in the basket and climbed in, Murdock cut the rope that was holding them, and the balloon rose slowly into the night air.

"Where did you get this thing?" Hannibal asked Murdock.

"The Face Man got it," said Murdock. "Get him talking – we need the hot air."

"An Armenian circus just docked," explained Face. "Some guy jumps out of it into a damp tissue."

"Great," said Hannibal. "Now all we need is a bottle of champagne."

There was the sound of a cork popping. Deadpan, Face handed Hannibal a bottle of ice cold champagne. Hannibal shook his head, gave a quiet chuckle and took a long drink.

"You don't want me to become a basket case, do you?" Murdock asked as Hannibal handed him the bottle.

"No, why?" asked Hannibal. "Is B.A. regaining consciousness?"

"As a matter of fact, he is," said Zoe, pointing upwards with her thumb. "And you'd better put out that cigar. The champagne cork punctured the balloon."

"Where am I?" groaned B.A. from the floor of the basket. "What's goin' on here? If you been jivin' me, Hannibal –"

"Would I?" asked Hannibal innocently, peering over the edge of the basket at the inky blackness below. "You've really got to watch that attitude. You know what they say."

"What do they say, sucker?"

"That the darkest hour . . . is just before everything goes completely black."

SEIZURE at SNEEKERVILLE

High up on the ridge, the Face Man studied the figure galloping towards them along the dusty mountain trail, then handed the binoculars to B.A.

"It's him," he said, fingering the remote control detonator in his hands. "You ready?"

"Not so fast, Face Man," growled B.A. "We got to wait for Murdock to make the pick up."

"Here he comes now," said Amy, pointing to an ancient crop-dusting bi-plane that had just swung into view round the lip of the cliff bordering the trail.

"And here come the bad guys," warned the Face Man. Rounding the trail some hundred yards behind the rider were three dark limousines, bucking over the rough terrain and sending clouds of dust into the air.

On board the bi-plane, Howling Mad Murdock abandoned his noisy imitation of Jimi Hendrix, cut his speed down to the absolute minimum, then grinned down at the hard pressed rider below. Under the telephone repairman's overalls and long black wig, the face of Hannibal Smith grinned right back up.

"All aboard for the moonshot!" yelled Murdock, taking the plane lower and throwing a rope ladder out of the side. Hannibal smoothly hopped up onto the back of the galloping horse, stood up briefly and leapt.

"Now!" shouted B.A. on the ridge.

The Face Man hit the button on the detonator, a huge rock on the cliffs disintegrated in a bright yellow ball of flame, and the sound of the explosion lost itself in the thundering avalanche that roared downwards, completely blocking the trail.

"Let's get out of here," said Amy, standing up and walking towards a jeep. B.A. kept the binoculars trained up at the sky.

"We got trouble," he said grimly. "The madman's taken a hit."

B.A. was right. The fuel line had been fractured during the chase and a small fire had started. Murdock had to find a place to land before it spread to the tanks.

"Know any good fly-in restaurants round here?" Murdock's voice was almost lost in the wind as he yelled at Hannibal. The A-Team number one was standing on the wing, fighting a losing battle with the fire.

"There's one," replied Hannibal, working the extinguisher as the bi-plane raced inches above the crest of a shrub covered hill, "but the Maitre d's got bad breath and there's no vowels in the alphabet soup."

"I knew I should have listened to momma," said Murdock. The plane crested another hill and the engine began spluttering. Below them a fast-moving river cut through the floor of a deep canyon.

"What did she say?" asked Hannibal. The engine cut out and the bi-plane went into a steep dive.

"Who?" Murdock fought to stop the bi-plane going into a terminal spin.

"Your momma!" Hannibal clung tighter to the struts as the water rushed up to meet them.

"You ain't my momma," said Murdock, pulling hard at the controls. "I hope you ain't trying to muscle in on my act, elephant man."

Suddenly, as the nose of the bi-plane began to lift and the frail craft started pulling out of its plunging dive, the wing Hannibal was standing on sheared off and he, the wing, Murdock and the rest of the crippled crop-duster splashed heavily into the boiling rapids of the mountain river.

It took an hour before the rest of the A-Team found the first signs of wreckage, a piece of wing jammed tight between two rocks. Beside it, stretched out like a skinned beaver, lay Hannibal's wig.

Amy felt hot tears spring from her eyes. B.A. put one of his huge arms round her shoulder and she buried her face against his jewellery.

"Do you think –" she sobbed.

"No, I don't!" B.A. said curtly. Face had picked up the wig and was removing a flat waterproof packet from the lining.

"We got the pictures anyway," he said, slipping the package into his belt.

Amy turned angrily. "Is that all you care about? They could be –"

"Dead," said the Face Man coolly. "Don't be afraid to say it, Amy. But we don't know, kid, and if they are alive they're gonna need us hanging loose – you got it?"

B.A. put his hand on her shoulder. "Face Man's right," he said softly. "An' don't worry – I ain't goin' to let anybody hurt you."

"I'm sorry," snuffled Amy, pulling a map from her pocket and spreading it out on the jeep. She followed the river's route with her finger. "Sneekerville's the next town," she said. "Maybe they've found something."

B.A., Amy and the Face Man drove towards Sneekerville on a narrow road that skirted the river. The only other wreckage they found was a large piece of propeller and a shoe. Face Man recognised it as Murdock's. They were still examining the shoe when they heard the first shots.

They turned and saw a tall, thin man in a sheriff's uniform ambling

towards them, a pump-action shotgun cradled idly in his arms. Behind him, six men in hunting jackets and caps aimed a variety of weapons in their direction.

"Before you get any big ideas, boys," said the Sheriff, "take a look behind you." The sheriff made a brief signal with one hand, and in the rocks across the river, several more heavily armed men stood up.

Face Man grinned. "That's great, sheriff," he said. He stepped forward and stood with his hands on his hips, examining his captors. "A little, er, clichéd perhaps – and I'm afraid the bimbo in the deerstalker will have to lose that corn-cob pipe, but if I didn't know better – I'd swear they were real people. Wouldn't you, Miss Tinderberry?"

"Of course," agreed Amy. She had no idea what the Face Man was trying to do.

"What are you talking about, boy?" The sheriff looked puzzled.

Face slapped his forehead with the palm of his hand. "Tinderberry – remind me to sack you as soon as I've squared this business with the governor. I'm sorry, sheriff – there's been a communications failure."

"You're beginning to get on my nerves, boy."

Face noticed several of the men in hunting jackets had moved closer. The man with the corn-cob was nearest of all. Face held up his hands.

"It's not your fault, boys," he said. "Believe me, I don't blame you. So what if a 25-mil boffo blockbuster goes down the tubes? Who cares if The Prettiest Little Town Of All never gets in the can? That's how it is with these whodunnits. They get to be more like 'what's going ons'. Don't you worry a –"

The Face Man was cut short by a blow to the chin with the butt of a hunting rifle. He fell to the floor unconscious, and Corn-cob, his attacker, snarled down at him.

"String him up," he said. "There's some rope in the truck."

B.A. moved forward. The sheriff stepped between them.

The relief at finding Hannibal and Murdock alive in the small Sneekerville jail was tempered by the fact that they were in trouble. Big trouble.

Murdock and Hannibal had been fished unconscious out of the river and immediately accused of kidnapping a busload of children on their way to the school in Dunchurch, the next, bigger town. The town of Sneekerville had been in uproar since the bus went missing, and several search parties had failed to find a single clue. It was as if the bus had been spirited away into thin air.

"There'll be no lynching while I'm in charge," he said. "These boys are going to jail until this thing's sorted out."

"Jail?" Amy's voice dripped with anger as she wiped the blood from Face Man's mouth. "On what charge?"

The sheriff spat onto the ground.

"The same as we got your two buddies on," he said slowly. "Kidnapping . . . and maybe murder."

"I had you figured as a man who wasn't quite so stupid as he looked," said Hannibal to the sheriff. The sheriff was staring out of his office window at the angry crowds of armed men who were gathering there. Hannibal was lying on his cell bunk.

"Just be quiet, boy," said the sheriff wearily.

"Haven't you even thought why anyone might want to kidnap a busload of schoolkids?" Hannibal went on.

"I've thought about it," the sheriff said. "But I can't figure it out."

"Let me give you a few of my ideas," began Hannibal.

But before he could continue there was a sudden commotion on the street outside, the door was kicked open, and Corn-cob came in, holding a hunting rifle in one hand and a child's red coat in the other.

"They found this in the woods by the old Jefferson place," he said. He placed it carefully down on the sheriff's desk and raised his rifle towards Hannibal. "You tell me what you've done with my girl or I'll blow your head clean off."

"I think you should find the right handle on this thing before you do that," said Hannibal, uncrossing his legs and sitting up to face his would-be killer. "Because if your child is in danger, we might be the only hope of saving her and the rest of the kids."

Corn-cob hesitated, looked across to the sheriff, then slumped down in a chair and began crying. The sheriff walked over and handed him a box of tissues.

"Don't worry, we'll find them," he said. "The military will be here soon."

"The military?" asked B.A., clutching the cell bars in sudden anger.

"Sure. A Colonel Lynch rang this morning to warn us he would be using the area to familiarise his men with mountain conditions."

"Colonel Lynch!?" B.A.'s biceps bunched and his knuckles paled against the black metal bars.

"Yeah, you know him?" asked the sheriff. Before B.A. could answer the door swung open again and another man entered wearing a hunting jacket.

"We're taking a search party up to the old Jefferson place. You coming?"

"Sure." Corn-cob shuffled out, leaving the A-Team alone with the sheriff.

Less than ten minutes after the search party pulled out, a jeep pulled up in front of the sheriff's office. The sheriff went out, spoke with the uniformed men in the jeep and then waved them off up the road. A large, covered army wagon followed down the main street.

Back inside, Amy spoke to the sheriff in a worried voice.

"You've got bigger trouble than you think, sheriff," she warned. "That man isn't Colonel Lynch."

"I've had just about enough, lady."

"Check my credentials. Ring up my boss – Grant Eldridge, *Courier-Express*. You've got bad trouble." Amy flashed her open wallet through the bars. The sheriff ignored it.

"She's right," agreed Hannibal. "I recognised that man. He was operating in Hanoi between '65 and '69. His name was Kurtz then. He's a vampire dingaling with a bad line in toytown politics and a very pressing need to dress up."

"Don't try to snow me." The sheriff was getting as confused as a hedgehog in a wig shop.

"At least give my boss a ring. I'll tell you the number."

"What would a terrorist want in a sleepy town like Sneekerville?" The sheriff seemed unable to take in exactly what was happening to him.

"Face up to it, sheriff," urged the Face Man. "Those kids were kidnapped so the whole town would be out of the way looking for them. Something's coming down and it can't be the bank – it's too small. What is it?"

"I know," said Amy. They all turned to listen. Amy shrugged her shoulders. "It's the reason why I was able to come along with you guys anyway. Eldridge wanted some background on how they transport them – security, that kind of thing."

"Transport what?" asked B.A.

Amy lowered her eyes. "Missile parts. There was a story that they're trying a new method of shifting them. Unmarked containers. Back roads. There'll be back-up, of course, but

low-profile's the name of the game."

"You reckon the missiles are coming through Sneekerville?" the sheriff asked.

Hannibal nodded. "And the reason we know so much about it is that the real Colonel Lynch is after us."

Somewhere in the sheriff's brain, the book of rules closed. He fetched the keys from the desk and opened the cell.

"I know I'm crazy, but I'm an American."

"So are we," said Hannibal. "Now here's what I want you all to do . . ."

"Don't forget my mother," interrupted Murdock. "She was two parts Martian."

Kurtz was feeling pleased with himself as he waited on the outskirts of town to halt the missile shipment. The kidnapping had gone without a hitch and the children were safe in the old barn miles from where he'd planted the clothing. By the time they were discovered it would be all over, and he would be very rich indeed.

As he saw the figure in the hunting jacket shuffling disconsolately towards him, corn-cob pipe alight, Kurtz drew his pistol. The man immediately raised his hands above his head. Kurtz felt a chill of fear race down his back when he saw, in the man's hand, the unmistakeable shape of a hand grenade.

"Bad to see you again, Kurtz," said Hannibal, abandoning his disguise and adopting an aggressive, threatening stance. "Drop it."

Kurtz laughed. Keeping his pistol trained on Hannibal he radioed the men and women he had sent off to their positions in readiness for the ambush. From the first he got no answer. From the second he got Howling Mad Murdock's imitation of an elephant seal being bitten by a shark. From the third and fourth, B.A. and Face Man answered with short, confident threats.

"See," said Hannibal with a smile. "Now pack up your marbles and go stand in the corner."

Kurtz cocked his pistol and sneered. "You forget that when you pull that pin I will still have enough time to kill you and get out of range," he said coldly.

Hannibal kept smiling and opened his palm so that Kurtz

could see that the pin from the grenade had already been pulled.

"I can't remember exactly how many seconds I counted," he smiled, "but I don't think there would be more than one single eeny-weeny second before the big sleep once I drop this thing."

"You're lying!"

"Am I?"

With a short laugh, Hannibal let the hand grenade fall. It rolled to Kurtz and stopped by his boots. The terrorist stared down as though it were a bag full of poisonous snakes: fascinated, horrified, unable to move.

. . . Until Hannibal's right hook sent him spinning to the ground. As Hannibal sauntered over to kick away Kurtz's gun, B.A.'s voice crackled over the airwaves.

"You alright, Hannibal? Remember, sucker, keep it simple. You know how you love the jazz."

Hannibal picked up the hand grenade and grinned. It was a soap one he had been fashioning in the Sneekerville jail to facilitate his escape. He pocketed it as the rest of the A-Team brought in their hostages.

"The kids are in a barn up on that hill," Hannibal told the sheriff, dragging Kurtz's unconscious body along the street towards the jail.

"And we've got what our original client was after," said Face, tapping his belt.

"You sure you won't stay around?" asked the sheriff. "You could help with the explanations."

Hannibal looked up at the sound of a large container wagon barrelling down the main street. At a discreet distance behind, a line of jeeps followed.

Hannibal grinned and saluted as the second jeep passed, with the real Colonel Lynch staring open-mouthed from the back seat.

"Some other time, sheriff," he said, leading the other members of the A-Team to Kurtz's jeep. "We gotta be going."

And with a squeal of rubber on tarmac and Murdock's, "Hi-yo Silver, awaaaaay!" they sped out of town as Lynch's men turned to give chase.

PLANE CRAZY!

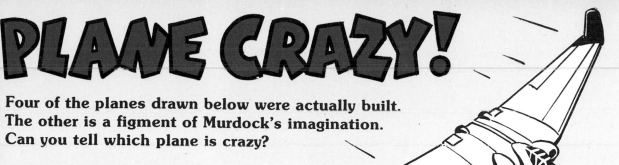

Four of the planes drawn below were actually built. The other is a figment of Murdock's imagination. Can you tell which plane is crazy?

1. The Flying Wing

This experimental plane made several flights and reached top speeds of around 500 m.p.h.

2. The Coleopter

This bizarre vertical take-off plane had circular wings wrapped all the way round the fuselage.

3. The Blom and Voss '141'

This unlikely looking craft carried three crewmen and could reach speeds in excess of 200 m.p.h.

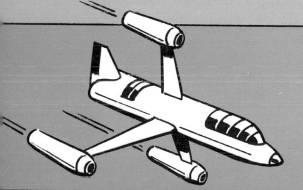

4. The Sukhoi '237'

This unusual plane had a top speed of 800 m.p.h. and carried a crew of six people.

5. The Chance–Vought XF59–1

This spectacular looking plane actually had a top speed of less than 500 m.p.h.

ANSWER: No. 4.

35

MURDOCK

He howls. He's mad. He plays unplugged videos. He's a mental aerobics master, flicking through his characters faster than a thief through a bankroll. He's even got a silly smirk — he tried a serious one once, but it didn't hang right. But fly? He could land a Jumbo Jet upside down with a roller skate on his head. And if for a moment anyone thought he was the slightest bit sane, he'd be back in Fort Bragg faster than a fly under a swatter. Murdock's crazy o.k. — like a fox.

FACE

You want it? Face can get it. From a peashooter to a Pershing II, from a catapult to a cruise missile – the Face Man can provide. Tarred and feathered, this Scholar of the Dollar could sell air-conditioning to eskimoes while juggling snow. And that famous visage? Coupled with a tongue so fast and slippery it could wrestle a snake, it has seen the A-Team through enough difficult moments to have turned it into something resembling an extremely sad prune. But, like a toothpaste ad-man on the make, the Face keeps on smiling.

DOWN AT THE DAY CARE CENTRE

B.A. spends a lot of his time at the Day Care Centre in Watts, helping the kids with their projects and steering them clear of trouble. But, despite his fearsome appearance, things don't always go his way . . . .

You SURE this is an authorised project?

Did you know there's exactly 33 muddy puddles on the way here?

Then again, the kids are always asking B.A. questions, especially about the military. In his own way, B.A. tells them everything he knows, stories that reflect the flip side of the tunes of glory . . . .

A high ranking officer noticed a sergeant giving a new recruit a particularly hard time.
"What's the matter with this man, Sergeant?" he asked.
"He's loudmouthed, rude and a liar," replied the Sergeant. "He called me a lily-livered, brainless twit, and I don't like it. I mean, how would you like to be called a stupid, lily-livered twit if you weren't one?"

The tough sergeant was inspecting his men when he noticed a faint stubble under one young man's nose.
"What's that?" he barked.
"My moustache, sir."
"Rub it out and start again."

A pilot was trying to take off in atrocious weather, watched by his instructor.
After two attempts down the rain-lashed runway he gave up.
"What's up?" asked the instructor. "Are you just a fair weather flier?"
"No, but when the altimeter registered six fathoms I thought it was time to surface."

Notice on cookhouse door:
It is true that bread is the staff of life, but that is no reason why the life of the staff should be one long loaf.

A soldier who had slipped out of camp for a night on the town tried to get back in by swinging over the fence on a rope hanging from a tree. He had planned to land on the roof of a hut, but the rope wasn't long enough, and as he swung from side to side above the fence the sergeant appeared.
"Breaking in, breaking out, breaking in, breaking out, breaking in . . ."

During parachute training one recruit was so far from the landing area that when he was asked to log his 'Distance From Target' he put 'Ten dollar cab ride'.

"Fire at will!" barked the C.O. as the enemy advanced.
"Which one's Will?" asked the new recruit.

Representatives of the Army, the Navy and the Air Force all gave speeches at a dinner. The Army and the Navy men, proud of their traditions, kept referring to the Air Force as the 'Cinderella' of the forces. When the Air Force man made his speech, he began with the lines: "I know very little about Cinderella — except that she had two ugly sisters."

The SCUZZBALL DIAMOND

The man at the bar looked ill-at-ease, and with good reason. He was out of place and well aware of the fact. Every now and then he would pull back the cuff of his expensively tailored shirt and glance at his gold wristwatch. It was 8.29 p.m.

They were late. The man on the stool next to him had fallen off it twice and now seemed to be getting angry about the emptiness of his glass. Philo P. Kirkman was getting the distinct impression that this wasn't going to be one of the better nights of his life.

And then a shrill, excited voice sounded in his ear.

"That face! That shape! That posture! The slight yellowing round the eyes! You, sir, are the most woefully ill-maintained specimen it has ever been my pleasure to see!"

"Unh?"

Philo turned to face the voice's owner, a wild-haired man with thick rimless spectacles and a huge grin, looking as happy as a baby beaver in a toothpick factory. He crossed the bar and peered deep into Philo's slate grey eyes.

"Such marvellous debilitation!" he said. "You do have trouble sleeping, don't you?"

As Philo made to nod, the man lifted Philo's lips and examined his teeth. He made strange noises at the back of his throat and then shone a light in Philo's ear.

"You'll be coughing a lot, of course, am I right?" he continued. "And that persistent little rash – it just won't go away, will it? Good! Excellent! My boy – I'm going to make you famous."

"Just what are you trying to pull?" Philo was getting angry.

The man ignored this fact. "Dr Olaf Von Trapp at your service," he said with a small bow. "Pioneering doctor. Your symptoms are really quite unique. You are just the man to prove my

"I'm a garlic salesman," said Murdock, grinning. "At least that's what it says on the inside of my cap. But that's just a cover. Really I'm a weapons system analyst working on a new bomb — it destroys everything except money."

"Shut your mouth, peanut head," B.A. warned.

Philo studied the three men, then turned to leave.

"I thought you wanted the A-Team?" said Hannibal.

"I want good men who can do a job for me, not a bunch of flakes."

Hannibal blocked Philo's way. He lit a cigar and then stared at the match until it went out.

"You first went looking for the A-Team three days ago," he said. "Since then you've spent a total of twenty eight and a half hours in your recording studio, twelve at your home, six and one quarter in transit, four in Martin's cocktail lounge where you tipped the waitress with two five dollar bills, serial numbers—"

"Okay! Okay!" Philo held up his hands. "You're good."

SET-TO

theory. I think I'll call it Von Trapp's Disease. What do you say?"

"I say button it, creep!" Philo was about to snap. Von Trapp soothed him by putting an arm round his shoulder.

"Of course, it means you don't have long to go, but never mind. You'll be famous and so will I. Together we will live side by side forever in the annals of medical history: Von Trapp . . . and his disease. What is your name, by the way?"

"I'm getting out of here," said Philo, trying to wriggle free.

Von Trapp's hand held firm, a glint of steel flashed in the wild

eyes, and the lips moved fast, framing the words that came in a clipped, urgent whisper.

"You wanna see the A-Team — follow me."

Philo did a quick double take as Von Trapp steered him towards the exit while resuming his manic diagnosis. Outside in the alley, B.A. was waiting by some crates with Howling Mad Murdock. B.A. stood against a wall with his arms crossed, while Murdock was playing with an imaginary yo-yo.

"Who are these guys?" asked Philo.

Von Trapp was too busy taking off his false beard to answer.

"You bet we're good," growled B.A. "You got the money?"

Philo nodded, drew an envelope from his jacket pocket and tossed it onto a crate. Hannibal picked it up and rifled quickly through the thick wad of crisp new high denomination notes.

"You just hired yourself some help."

Philo took out a photograph and showed it to Hannibal. It showed four young men dressed in identical leather suits.

"The Doom Watchers," explained Philo. "They've got my baby."

"What's the baby called?" asked Hannibal.

"Undersea Motion."

"Makes a change from Sam, I suppose," said Murdock.

"It's not a real baby, pinhead," said Philo. "It's the master tapes to my new record."

"Why don't you just call the cops?" Hannibal asked.

"The record needs to come out now," said Philo. "And I can't spend two years dragging those creeps through the courts."

"You got any proof the tapes are yours?"

Philo rose to his full height of 5 feet 2 inches. He puffed out his chest like a pigeon.

"Proof?" he said indignantly. "You ask me, Philo P. Kirkman, for proof? The man who wrote *Skooby Dibby Goo-Goo?* The creator of the immortal *Wings of Change?* Sole writer, singer and producer of that greatest of all pop classics, *Gimme, Gimme, Gimme?*"

"That's right," said Hannibal.

Philo took out a document from his pocket. "This is a binding legal contract signed by all the parties concerned."

"The writing's a little small."

"You want a photograph of the handshake?"

"Okay – you know where these guys can be reached?"

"They're squatting at an old movie ranch out in the desert mountains."

"Ain't that where Death's Drivers hang out?" asked B.A.

"The motor cycle gang? That's right," said Philo. "They're the Doom Watchers' unofficial fan club and bodyguards."

"They're bad cats, Hannibal," said B.A.

"So are we, Sergeant," Hannibal replied. "So are we."

The following night, while the rest of the A-Team made their own preparations for the mission, the Face Man, dressed in a sleeveless denim jacket and heavy motorcycle boots, tooled into the Death's Drivers camp on a

gleaming Harley Davidson he had fast talked from a hire purchase company. B.A. had spent the day making special modifications to the powerful machine.

As Face eased off the throttle, one of the Death's Drivers came out to meet him. He had the kind of face ancient stonecutters carved to ward off demons. On top of his long dirty hair he wore a Viking helmet with two long horns.

"Ever get a sudden urge to go 'MOOOOOO!'?" asked Face.

"I see you ain't wearing any colours — what chapter are you with?" asked a girl who had come out of the shack and was eyeing Face's bike greedily. She stood 4 feet 11 inches and wore the legend GIANT on her grease-covered overalls.

"Independent — The Scuzzball Diamonds," said Face.

The man and Giant laughed so long and loud that other bikers came out of the ranch house to see what was happening.

"Any of you guys heard of the Scuzzball Piemen?" asked Giant.

"Diamonds," corrected Face. "The Scuzzball Diamonds."

Face's words set off another round of wild laughter. The Viking, tears streaming down his face, stepped forward.

"Before we find out what you want, we find out what you are," he said. "How do you like jousting?"

"I like that fine," said Face.

A cheer went up from the Death's Drivers. Face noticed that four members of the Doom Watchers were standing on the porch.

The old movie ranch was built by a disused mine, and outside the mine entrance the Death Drivers lined up with flaming torches to form a narrow corridor for the Viking and Face to duel. They were each given one long stave, and they faced each other some fifty yards apart, engines revving, waiting for the signal to start.

"Now!" said Giant.

The Viking's bike reared up like a horse that has stepped on a rattler, and by the time he had got

his weight forward he was nearly on top of the Face Man. Face was still trying to balance his stave when the Viking's weapon caught him on the shoulder, and he was sent flying backwards from his machine.

The Viking held his stave up in triumph as he circled for the next attack. Face scrambled after his stave, then turned to defend himself. When the Viking's bike was nearly on him, he sidestepped neatly, lashed downward with his stave, and buried the other man's weapon into the ground.

Like a jet propelled pole-vaulter, the Viking flew through the air, over the heads of the other Death's Drivers, and straight towards a small coal truck at the mine's entrance.

The impact of his bulk smashing into the truck sent it rolling into the mine, with the Viking as the cargo. There was a rumbling sound, a sharp crash, and then, long seconds later, a distant splash. Giant looked at Face with new respect.

"How d'you get to be so old being so stupid?" she asked. "It will take him hours to climb out of there. I reckon you're ready for a bigger test."

"More jousting?" asked Face. "I'd love to oblige you and all that, but I think I'm getting a touch of jouster's elbow."

"This is a straight forward chicken-run," said Giant. "Between you and me."

"If you insist," said Face, retrieving his bike, as Giant disappeared into a huge barn. The deep rumbling of powerful engines from inside the barn made him wonder what a turkey felt like as December grew close.

The door to the barn opened and a truck trundled out, took off up the track, turned, and raced towards the Face Man. Face gunned his engine and raced to meet the challenge.

As the massive truck bore down on the Harley Davidson, Face was thinking fast. There was no way he could do a controlled slide under the truck. There was no way he could do very much at all, really, except . . . .

Face did a wheelie, checked his speed, and with the thundering truck only yards away, activated the retro rockets B.A. had fitted to his machine. For one terrifying fraction of a second it seemed like they weren't going to work.

And then, with a full-throated howl the rockets ignited, the Harley Davidson took off, bounced off the roof of the trailer, and landed upright on the dirt road behind.

As Face struggled to control the bike a great cheer went up among the Death's Drivers, and when Face rode back, all of them, including Giant, crowded round his machine like starving dogs round a leg of lamb.

"Maybe now we can talk," said Face. "It's about Philo P. Kirkman."

One of the Doom Watchers picked up the Viking's abandoned stave.

"If you're from that bucket of ancient swill, you won't be going back in one piece!" he warned, lifting the stave above his head.

"Do I take it that you and Philo have some misunderstanding?" asked Face.

"Sure – he ripped us off good. Stole our music and paid us off with phoney bills. If it hadn't been for the Death's Drivers we'd have never got our tapes back."

"I thought you'd signed a contract," Face observed

"Sure – for real money. Once he slipped us the dud cash it was null and void."

"You're quite a lawyer for a pop star."

"The question is, jumping bean," said Giant, "just what are you going to do about it?"

The Face Man listened to the distant whine of motor cycles racing up the trail.

He saw the lights of the helicopter above them. The rest of the Scuzzball Diamonds were coming in as planned.

"That's a very good question," he said.

The fight that followed would have livened up most of the films shot at the old ranch. B.A. gave his impression of a heavyweight

champion grizzly bear, and Hannibal – cigar clenched firmly in his teeth – slugged it out back to back with the Face Man.

Sue and Murdock livened up the proceedings by buzzing the farm in their helicopter, dropping 'flares, small explosive charges, and the kind of gas grenade used to flush rats out of ships.

When the smoke cleared, Face lay groaning on the ground, B.A. was trapped inside a water barrel and Hannibal was being sat on by the newly wet, resurfaced Viking.

"I love it when a plan comes together," said Hannibal.

"I told you this plan was crazy!" snapped B.A.

Face staggered to his feet, rubbing a purplish scar on his cheekbone. "There's been a mix-up," he said.

"I know," said Hannibal. "I checked the bills Kirkman gave us."

"But why?" asked Face.

Hannibal grinned.

"You and that jazz, man!" scowled B.A. "You gonna get us killed one day!"

"You've got to improve that attitude, B.A.," said Hannibal. "And if this horned toad would get off me, I could signal Murdock down and tell you what we're going to do . . ."

Philo P. Kirkman was relaxing in the luke-warm, salt-impregnated water of his private isolation tank when Hannibal turned up wearing a pin-striped suit. He was also sporting black hair dye, a thin black moustache, and a black Homburg. He was carrying a box full of tapes. He opened Philo's tank and threw in a towel. Philo came out,

At that moment B.A. opened his eyes and began to struggle against the straps holding him down on the stretcher. Hannibal pulled the sheet back over his head.

"What the heck's I.U.P?" asked the customs man.

Hannibal remained cool. "It's the er . . . Institute of Unexplained Phenomena – top secret. It's an urgent case."

The customs man pulled back the top of the blanket and backed away from B.A.'s ferocious glare.

"We found him in a block of ice," Murdock interrupted. "If we don't get him to our special isolation unit before he thaws out completely it could mean trouble – germs and things. We'll have to use your car."

From the stretcher, B.A. growled with frustration and anger.

"Who . . . what exactly is it?" asked the customs man.

"Don't call him the missing link," warned Murdock, "even though he might well be that final piece of the jigsaw of evolution, the vacant page in our knowledge of the evolutionary chain, the blind spot in our historical vision between the Plasticene era and the age of plastic dinos – AAARGH!" B.A. had worked one hand free from the straps and was grasping Murdock round the throat. Using all his strength, Face managed to unlock the grip.

"It might be too late already," he said, helping Ann load B.A. into the back of an ambulance. "We'll bring this back when we've finished."

Hannibal climbed into the driving seat, ignoring the suspicious, bemused stares. "And in the meantime, make sure the tanks are full and the aircraft is ready to fly." With that, he gunned the motor and drove out of the airport and onto the busy highway.

Carolyn Kent, the A-Team's client, had watched the proceedings with a growing feeling of alarm. When Murdock climbed out of the window onto the roof of the speeding ambulance to escape B.A.'s temper, she finally snapped.

"Stop the ambulance!" she screamed. "This is madness!"

Hannibal brought the ambulance to a quick stop and Murdock slid off the roof onto the bonnet.

"You want out – there's the door," said Hannibal. "You want us to save your father's life – we'll do it our way."

Carolyn tossed her head and her long blonde curls shook free of her heart-shaped face. Hannibal could

back at him.
"All right," she said. "Let's go and see Teeny."

Teeny was an artist who lived in a shack near the huge walled mansion where Carolyn's father was being held, deep in a valley near the Kamehame ridge. Teeny sculpted in metals, and he was working on a piece entitled 'Helmet', when Hannibal, Carolyn, Murdock and B.A. arrived.

He switched off his oxy-acetylene torch and pulled up his visor. "The most beautiful of all shapes didn't come out of nature, you know," he said. "The most sublime contours the world has seen are found in the rudimentary shape of the steel helmet."

"Absolutely," said Hannibal. "How many gas tanks have you got?"

"About six," said Teeny. "Such solid, reliable and friendly things, don't you agree?"

"Absolutely," repeated Hannibal. "You mind if we look around?"

"Not at all," said Teeny. "Perhaps your friend might be interested in some jewellery."

see why she earned 3,000 dollars a day as a fashion model.

"The people who've got my father are very well organised," she said. "They've got people working for them throughout the Hawaiian Islands. They work hand in glove with some of the biggest criminal organisations on the mainland. They are an extremely effective and sophisticated outfit."

Hannibal's face broke open in an easy grin.

"And we're the bell-boys at the Hotel Screwball!"

"Well . . ." Carolyn's voice trailed off as she surveyed the A-Team. Ann and Face were smiling, Murdock was whispering into his shoe and B.A. maintained his customary ferocious glare, like a bulldog whose dinner has been stolen by the cat.

"We'll get your father, lady," said B.A. gruffly. "We'll give the bad guys pain. All this stuff is just Hannibal's style. He loves the jazz, man. He just loves the jazz."

Carolyn remained unconvinced.

"There's one other thing . . ." she said. "This is not your usual bunch of strong-arm goons with stolen cars backing up on their drives. The reason this set-up runs so well is because the person running it is smart."

"Ain't no man smarter than Hannibal," said B.A. "Exceptin' myself."

"This ain't no man," said Carolyn. "The boss of this outfit is a woman."

"So am I," said Ann.

The two women held each other's gaze until Murdock handed Carolyn his shoe.

"It's for you," he said.

Carolyn grinned and threw it

"Perhaps he might be," said Hannibal, leading B.A. into the shack. Piled round the walls were bits of scrap metal of all shapes and sizes. To the untrained eye it was just junk, but to B.A. it was a treasure trove.

Hannibal smiled appreciatively and placed his arm round Teeny's shoulder.

"As you can probably see," he said, "my friend here is something of an artist as well. He is a long time admirer of your work and has expressed a strong desire to work with you on a combined project."

"What kind of project?" asked Teeny.

Hannibal's eyes fixed on an imaginary horizon and he waved his hands expansively in the air. "I see it as a big project. A meeting of minds, of man and machine, a concept so daring, so potent, so awesome, that the minds of men will reel from its dazzling, incandescent brilliance."

"Like 'Helmet'?" asked Teeny.

Hannibal nodded. "Exactly like 'Helmet'. But different. This thing will be so good it will put Michaelangelo back with the shipping news. It's called . . . 'Gun'."

"I like it! I like it!"

"I thought you might. O.K., B.A., let's get this show on the road."

While Hannibal was organising things at Teeny's place, Ann and the Face Man were being escorted round the back of the mansion that was Carolyn's father's jail. What they saw was not encouraging . . .

A barbecue was being held by the swimming pool. Several

hard-looking men jogged round the pool in tracksuits. There were two men in black suits guarding every door. In the pool, lounging on inflatable plastic armchairs, three men sat round a floating table headed by a beautiful blonde-haired woman in her early thirties. Ann recognised her at once from her newspaper files: Stella Stanforth, the fastest rising star in the criminal firmament.

She gave a brief nod and two of the men slipped off their inflatable chairs and pushed them to the side of the pool for Face and Ann to climb on. Face refused.

"What's the matter, was your mother frightened by a glass of water?" the man asked.

"No, it's not that," smiled Face. "I used to be in the navy. I had a bad time."

"What happened?"

"Well, er . . . we were three weeks out of Nantucket when we ran into some icebergs. Boat got squashed to bits. We had to rig up sails on the berg and sail her right back to port. By the time we got back there were six of us sharing a piece of ice so small we had to order more for our celebration drinks."

Face felt the pressure of a gun against his back. He and Ann climbed onto the inflatable chairs and paddled over to where Stella was sipping a Mai Tai.

"What exactly do you two want?" she asked.

"We represent the interests of an appliance repair company," said Ann briskly. "Did you know that the appliance repair field is so uncrowded that it's almost lonely? The room for growth is phenomenal. We're running a scheme whereby –"

"You break the law for money," Stella interrupted. "You can drop the act now. You two are from the A-Team."

"What?" asked Face. "Are you trying to be funny?"

"I know all about you, Face – or should I say Templeton? And you too, Ann. You're both here to try and spring that nosey reporter I've got stashed away – right?"

Face shrugged.

Stella put her Mai Tai down on the floating table and drew a small silver pistol from her bag.

"It so happens that I like you guys," she said. "That stunt you pulled in San Rio Blanco was a real class act. How'd you like to work for me?"

Ann and Face exchanged glances.

"Aw, c'mon," said Stella.

"We're all in the same racket, even though you try to come on like Robin Hood. We're all here to milk the suckers."

The Face Man's expression hardened. To have the A-Team compared with a gang of vicious hoodlums hurt his pride.

"Anyway," said Stella, her neatly manicured finger squeezing round the trigger, "you either say yes or you die."

The first gas cylinder came hissing over the mansion walls under its own steam, fired from B.A.'s 'Gun' near Teeny's house. It scored a direct hit on the barbecue fire, smashed open on the marble tiles and sent a roaring ball of flame high into the air.

Stella hesitated, and Face used the split second to unplug his inflatable chair. As the chair sped

"Over here!" yelled Hannibal, leaning out of the passenger seat and loosing off a short burst from his machine gun.

As Ann and Face raced for the safety of the bus, Hannibal turned to Murdock, who was crouching on the top of the bus aiming a cross-bow at an upstairs window. "Go!" Hannibal ordered.

Murdock fired the crossbow and a canister trailing strong nylon line smashed through the upstairs window. Within seconds they could see the shadowy figure of Carolyn's father as he secured the line and grabbed hold of a pulley to slide down. Murdock fastened the other end to a loop bolted onto the roof of the bus, and Hannibal signalled for Mr Seymour to slide down.

Although the gangsters had recovered from their shock and had taken up firing positions throughout the luxurious gardens, Carolyn's father landed unhurt on the roof of the bus and was quickly bundled inside.

"All aboard who's going aboard," said Hannibal. "Let's go, B.A."

As the gangsters closed in on them B.A. gunned the engine. It stalled. Hannibal, Murdock and Face tried to drive the gangsters back with more fire, but none of them could stop one hood throwing a can of petrol over the reinforced bus.

"C'mon, B.A.," said Face. "If that stuff catches we're going to fry."

"Don't push me, Face Man," warned B.A., "or you ain't gonna be so pretty, dig?" He tried the engine again. It was dead.

"I don't want to alarm you unduly," Murdock said in the clipped authoritative tones popularised by English war films. "But someone's lit the trail of petrol."

Hannibal looked out of the window. Murdock was right. The trail of petrol had been lit and the flames were racing along it towards the petrol-soaked bus. They were almost licking the back bumper when the engine fired.

crazily round the pool, Ann picked out the cocktail stick from Stella's drink and drove it deep into the arm of the crime queen's chair. She then unplugged her own.

The second and third cylinders were not so well aimed as the first, but they succeeded in spreading even more panic and confusion among the gangsters. The first smashed through the mansion's ornate French windows and the other landed in the pool itself, sending a continuous high pressure jet of water spraying round the poolside.

Face slid off his rapidly sinking chair and grabbed hold of Stella.

"You'd better kill me," she spluttered, "because I ain't gonna forget this."

Face wrestled the pistol from her hand and swam to the edge of the pool.

"Kill them both!" Stella raged at her henchmen, who were too busy trying to put out fires to know what was happening. They didn't even see the armour-plated bus coming until it smashed through the mansion's metal gates and screeched to a halt by the pool.

B.A. threw the bus into gear, and with tyres squealing and spinning, headed back for the smashed gates. The bus brushed aside a Ferrari that was blocking the drive and soon they were racing past the Halona Blowhole Lookout and heading for Highway One.

As Carolyn and her father hugged each other happily in the back of the bus, B.A. eased off the throttle.

"Where to, Hannibal?" he asked. "The docks?"

"Yes, er . . . that way at least. Why?"

"Because this place is an island and I ain't goin' on no airplane!"

"Take it easy, B.A.," said Face. "You might hurt Murdock's feelings."

"I ain't flying with that crazy fool!"

"Be careful what you say, B.A.," said Ann. "It might unbalance Murdock's state of mind."

"Quite," said Murdock, laboriously counting his fingers.

"I've had enough of your foolish rap," said B.A., bringing the bus to a halt under some palm trees. "I told you I ain't goin' on no airplane!"

Hannibal made a show of swatting a fly on his neck. B.A. grabbed him by the arm and pulled him close.

"Don't try that mosquito routine, sucker!" He forced Hannibal to open his hand. There was a small swab of cotton wool there. "This is the last time,

Hannibal! I ain't goin' in the air with that crazy man. If he flies, we die! I ain't goin' in no airplane even if I have to sit here for the rest of my life!"

But B.A. didn't sit there long, for when he had grabbed Hannibal, Ann had taken advantage of the argument to administer the powerful sleeping draught that was the only way the A-Team could get B.A. into an airplane. He mumbled twice, and then slumped forward with his forehead on the horn. Hannibal lifted him gently out of the driver's seat.

"Now we've only got one problem," he said, starting the motor up.

"What's that?" asked Ann.

"How the heck we're gonna talk ourselves back on that plane!"

Get . . . The A-Team

Ten years ago, a crack group of Marine Commandoes was sentenced by a military court for a crime they did not commit.

These men promptly escaped from the maximum security stockade to the Los Angeles underground.

Today, still wanted by the government, they survive as soldiers of fortune.

If you have a problem that no one else can solve, and if you can find them, maybe you can hire . . . THE A-TEAM.

But how do you find them? Los Angeles is a huge, sprawling city packed with all kinds of oddballs, and the only certainty is that once you start looking for the A-Team, the A-Team will be looking at you, checking you out as a potential client.

See who can get to all the members of the A-Team first.

CAR CHASE – THROW AGAIN

FACE

A game for two or more players.

If a player lands on a space containing instructions, they must be obeyed.

Players may move in any direction they like, but cannot turn back in the middle of a throw.

The winner is the first player to land on all the spaces containing a picture of an A-Team member and then return to the start.

STOP TO GAWP AT FILM STAR – MISS A THROW

GET DIRECTIONS TO V.A. HOSPITAL – THROW AGAIN

B.A.

62